Blast From the Past

Matthew Loehle

Published with permission of the author by
KidPub Press
www.kidpub.com

First printing June, 2009

Printed in USA

Dedicated to my family, and to the Laplaca family, and to my fifth-grade classmates.

- Matthew Loehle, 2009

Acknowledgments

I do not know how this book would have come about without the help of three of my teachers from St. Mary of the Annunciation School in Danvers, Massachusetts: Mrs. Judy LePage, my third grade teacher; Mrs. Kara Berry, my fourth grade reading teacher; and Mrs. Maureen Demsey, my fifth grade reading teacher. They have given me the tools, confidence and encouragement to write this book.

I would like to give a special thank you to Mrs. Demsey for taking her time to help me edit this book. I would also like to thank Mary Beth Laplaca for showing me the story she wrote and inspiring me to write this book. Finally, I would like to thank my family for their help and support while writing this book.

Contents

Magazines

A voice rang out over the intercom.

"Good morning, orphans, this is your dorm monitor speaking! Please report to the cafeteria in the next three and a half minutes."

Andrew rolled over in bed and grumbled, "Can't a kid get some sleep around here?"

Three minutes later, he was in the gray and dismal cafeteria, sitting on a gray and dismal bench, staring at his unappetizing gray and dismal mush. His one and only friend, Jerry Martin, sat down beside him.

"Whassup, Andy?"

With a grumble, he replied, "as usual, nuthin'. Wha' do you expect? We've been doing the exact same thing for the past nine years! By the way, what did you get on your math test?"

"I got a 56. Not much better than you, I suspect."

Before Andrew could reply, a young orphan came running into the cafeteria interrupting everyone. "Did ya hear about what's going on upstairs? A pretty lady just walked in and I think she's gonna adopt one of us!" the boy panted breathlessly. Andrew and Jerry exchanged looks. "But you guys shoulda seen – there was this guy in a wheelchair with her!" the boy continued. "Seriously dude, who would wanna be adopted by a guy in a wheelchair?" A few kids made faces and nodded in agreement.

"Hey Andrew," Jerry said over all the chaos, "don't ya think it would be cool if we got adopted? I mean both of us."

"What are the odds of that happening?" Andrew snorted.

Jerry shrugged, "It could happen." Andrew shook his head, changing the subject.

"Oh, Jerry, did you hear the rumor going around about a field trip?"

"No. What class?"

"Social studies. Pretty odd, don't ya think? That Ms. Allard doesn't know nuthin' about field trips," Andrew said quietly, trying not to let anyone nearby hear.

Andrew and Jerry talked on until the intercom interrupted them and Mr. Baker, the director of the orphanage, greeted them.

"Please report to your classrooms. You have exactly one and a quarter minutes. Thank you." Andrew and Jerry gathered up their books and headed off to their first class, social studies.

When they got there, the two boys met with a surprise. The social studies teacher and assistant director, Ms. Allard, was wearing a raincoat instead of her usual gray sweater. She announced, "Today, class, we are going on a field trip. Please return to your dorms and retrieve your coats."

Andrew glanced at Jerry, as if to say: *Told you!*

Hurrying back, Andrew grabbed his poncho and the sock full of loose change he had kept for special occasions.

Outside, it was a rainy summer day. However, the class was thrilled to be outside. This was the first time they had been outside the walls of the orphanage in a very long time. The last time, Andrew recalled staring at a television screen in a store, watching a baseball game. From that day, he was hooked. He talked about baseball every day with Jerry, and with the kids passing by his window. He could tell you the stats of any player, on any team, in the past three years. But most of all, he loved the Yankees.

In the distance, he heard a rumble of thunder, hauling him back into the present. Ms. Allard led them to the entrance of the subway system. Pointing to the ceiling of the station, she said, "Does anyone recall who decorated the ceiling of this station from our lesson yesterday? How about you, Mr. MacLean?" She pointed at Andrew.

He stood there for a moment, his mouth dry as a bone.

"I- I don't know, ma'am," he stammered nervously.

"Didn't any of you remember the lesson from yesterday? How about you, Jerry?"

"Um, miss, you didn't give us a lesson yesterday. You had us write an essay on the Byzantine Empire."

"Well, well, Mr. Martin, we don't need a smart mouth. Detention, tomorrow in my office. You too, Mr. MacLean. Did any of you do the assignment?"

"Ma'am, you didn't give us a lesson," everyone replied timidly.

"You're all liars! Detention, all of you! I am reporting this to Mr. Baker!" she screeched, as her face turned a shade of green usually associated with pond scum. Andrew and Jerry exchanged looks. As Ms. Allard primly lead the way, Andrew noticed a vendor selling copies of Sports Illustrated. He quickly put some money on the man's table and grabbed a copy, hiding it under his damp, torn shirt.

"Where did you get that?" Jerry whispered, barely audible.

"Saved up pennies that I found 'round the orphanage," Andrew whispered back, while he ran his fingers through his straw blond hair, which was now soaked with water. The field trip ended quickly as they headed back to the orphanage.

In Trouble

Once they got back, Andrew and Jerry clambered up to their dormitory. They jumped onto a bed and ripped out the magazine. As Andrew desperately flipped page by page, Jerry talked about the stars, like Derek Jeter, Alex Rodriguez, and Jorge Posada.

On and on they went, laughing at each other's jokes and chatting. They probably would have gone on forever if it were not for Mr. Baker. It all happened very quickly. He came down the hall, his shoes squeaking like mice on the marble floor. Andrew and Jerry knew that sound anywhere. They fumbled with the magazine to hide it under the gray, scratchy, pillow. The door banged open and Mr. Baker stormed in. His round, pig-like face had a tint of purple as he glared at the two of them.

"Now, you two" Mr. Baker said tensely, trying to keep his temper under control. "Please make my job easy, and tell me politely how you happen to come by that... that... dreadful magazine."

Andrew's heart was stuck in his throat.

"I- I... well... sort of ..."

"He bought it from a vendor, using money that wasn't his," Jerry interrupted, apparently sneering. Andrew was stunned and confused. His only friend was snitching on him! One minute he's laughing and having a good time, then the next minute he was turning him in! He felt his friendship shatter into a million pieces.

"Thank you, Jerry. In my office, Mr. MacLean."

Andrew sulked behind Mr. Baker. Looking back, Jerry mouthed something to him. Andrew felt complete disgust.

"So, my friend. Tell me. Why did you take this, Andrew?" Mr. Baker inquired when they were back in his office. He seemed nervous, but calm at the same time. For some odd reason, his chubby fist was whitened as he clenched tightly to his desk drawer. It caught Andrew's attention, and Mr. Baker noticed. He let his grip loosen as Andrew spoke.

"Um, well... it's a long story, and, you know, you wouldn't want to listen to my story forever..."

Mr. Baker's beady eyes quickly told Andrew that he wasn't buying it this time.

6

"Andrew MacLean. I do not play silly childish games anymore. I would very much like for you to tell…"

The ringing of the loud doorbell suddenly interrupted Mr. Baker.

"Excuse me, Mr. MacLean. Wait here until I'm finished, thank you very much."

The minute Andrew saw Mr. Baker leave, he darted off to the drawer. He was still suspicious about why Mr. Baker was holding the drawer so tightly. Desperately, Andrew opened it. His eyes widened with amazement.

Gone

*A*ndrew took a yellowed newspaper out of the drawer. Why was Mr. Baker trying to hide this old newspaper clipping? His question was quickly answered by looking at the first headline he saw.

It read:

BLAST FROM THE PAST

"'Blast From the Past'? What?" Andrew had all these questions bouncing off his brain. He was only able to skim it, but he understood.

The baseball field in Boston was discovered to possess spirits of some sorts. However, Andrew knew it was just some bogus box of lies. Definitely, it was just some janitor who heard stuff in his head. Big whup.

Thinking a bit more, Andrew chuckled to himself to think that there might be 'spirits' in Yankee Stadium (which happened to be in New York, across town from the orphanage).

Andrew quickly slammed the frail newspaper back into the drawer at the sound of polished shoes squeaking on a marble floor. He hurriedly shut it just before Mr. Baker marched in.

"What were you just doing?" Mr. Baker asked, staring at the half-closed drawer. Andrew's stomach did a cartwheel.

"Nothing," Andrew replied weakly. Mr. Baker's gray mustache twitched, and his gray hair got a bit grayer.

"Back to your dorm," Mr. Baker said briskly. "And stay in your dorm for the rest of the day."

The three hours Andrew waited were the longest hours ever. He sat, and sat, and sat. Finally, to his relief, a trembling voice on the intercom buzzed.

"All orphans, please report to the cafeteria for dinner in the next two-and-a-half minutes. Thank you."

Andrew groggily slid out of his uncomfortable bed. He glanced at the clock. 5:45 p.m. as usual.

Andrew joined a group of small orphans headed down to the café. They were all chattering loudly to each other, and Andrew was getting a headache.

"Hush, children," a nearby teacher scolded sternly. The little kids stared at her, as if to say, "What?"

At the cafeteria, he sat alone, which was very unusual. Andrew's stale spaghetti seemed to look back at his own depressed face.

He glanced over behind him to see Jerry laughing with another orphan named Ian. Andrew gritted his teeth. He just couldn't take it any more. Andrew got up, dumped his spaghetti in the trash, and stormed up to his dorm.

He jumped onto his scratchy bed, outraged. There was nothing for him here, in this heap of an orphanage. He had no family, no cousins, and now no friends. Andrew's eyes were stinging with tears, but he had to hold them back. He wasn't going to let Jerry make him cry like a two-year-old. Clutching a photo against his empty chest, Andrew started to cry. He never liked to cry as a baby nor as a kid, for it just wasn't his nature. However his tears streamed down his face, and splashed onto the photograph of his lost family.

All Andrew could do was lie down on his bed. He knew that crying wouldn't fix anything.

His bed seemed to stiffen, as if someone put a wooden board under the mattress. Still, he managed to finally fall asleep.

Andrew woke abruptly by the sound of mice clawing inside the wall. It was still dark out, to Andrew's disappointment.

He was about to go back to sleep when an idea struck him. Why was he here? He had no friends or family, so why stay here? And with his 'best friend' gone, Jerry would realize how mean and rotten he was to Andrew!

"Yes," thought Andrew. "I'm done here!" With that, Andrew hopped out of bed and slipped over to his pile of dirty clothes. He grabbed a T-shirt and a couple of jeans to keep him somewhat warm.

Andrew had made up his mind. He was leaving. For good.

Holding his sock full of loose change, a few pieces of clothing, and a book, he quickly jumped out the nearby window Mr. Baker had opened to let cool air into the dorm.

Andrew landed swiftly on the dark, cold ground. The holes in his torn shoes allowed the water to wet his socks, which made him quite uncomfortable. He looked back at the orphanage one last time.

"See ya, Jerry," Andrew muttered. Swiftly, Andrew darted to the first tree he saw.

After walking a little while, Andrew decided to take a rest before continuing in the morning. He stopped by a gnarly old tree that had started to rot by its humongous roots.

"This ought to be a good place to rest," Andrew thought, laying out his worn T-shirt on one of the roots.

Tossing and turning, Andrew tried desperately to get some rest. Not knowing how on earth he managed it, but yes, he was finally able, with difficulty, to get to sleep.

Pickpocket

*A*ndrew woke suddenly by the sound of screeching cars zooming by, not the buzzing of an intercom as he had expected. Groggily, Andrew stood up, wiping sleep out of his sunken eyes. His blonde hair was now a tangled mess, while his face was smeared with dirt and mud.

Gathering his shirt and other 'supplies' Andrew set off once again. Though his skinny legs were stiff and sleepy, he managed to walk it off.

Andrew soon realized what a gamble he was taking. What if he didn't make it to wherever he was going? How would he get food?

Most of all, what was happening at the orphanage? Would Mr. Baker call the police? Andrew shuddered and kept walking. The thoughts just haunted him constantly. But would Mr. Baker do something like that?

"No," Andrew told himself firmly. "Mr. Baker wouldn't do anything like that." However, on the inside, Andrew had a feeling that someone would report on a missing orphan.

Thinking about it just made it worse. Andrew was fighting with himself, not realizing a huge shadow had recently cast over him.

Andrew froze. He looked up to find a gigantic building overhead. Petrified, Andrew felt as if he was the size of a bug compared to the giant brick walls.

On second thought, Andrew felt bewildered. What building was it? There are so many buildings in modern-day New York City. Andrew couldn't find the correct name for it until he saw a worn sign. It read:

Yankee Stadium
Home of the New York Yankees

Andrew's eyes were as round as walnuts. This was the home of his heroes!

He saw the lines of people stretching around the building. There was a big poster announcing the afternoon's Yankees versus Boston Red Sox game.

Near the end of the line, a man caught his attention. He was a tall man wearing a Goth tee shirt, his neck jangling with black stones. He walked up to a young, attractive brown haired lady, embracing her.

"Ruth! I haven't seen you in three years! How's Laurie?"

Andrew barely heard this over the roar of the impatient crowd. However, he recognized the technique as he remembered when he was at the orphanage. He and Jerry would always look out the orphanage window and Jerry would point out the buildings in the distance, while Andrew's attention would be on the streets of New York. There would usually be people bumping into unsuspecting citizens, secretly taking a wallet, jewelry or whatever they could get. Eventually, the victim would realize their wallet or watch had disappeared. That is when it hit Andrew: The man hugging the brown haired lady was a pickpocket. This was the basic move.

The woman started to reply, "Who are…"

"Oops! I thought you were someone else," he interrupted, backing away, a brown leather rectangle hidden in his grasp.

Andrew raced toward the man. He took a big leap, landing squarely on the unwitting thief. He stumbled and crashed to the ground, Andrew on his back.

Andrew looked up, staring into the eyes of the crowd control officer peering down at him. "I can explain…" he said.

"Save the explanation, sonny."

"But look! He stole that lady's wallet!" That perked up the officer.

He walked with Andrew over to the woman, showing her the wallet. She gasped and thanked Andrew.

"I… I…," the woman was looking for the words to use, but she couldn't find them. "Thank y-you!" Andrew nodded, and walked off.

"Wait!" the lady shouted before Andrew could take another step. She hurried towards him, her silky brown hair flying behind her. "My name is Estella Lewis. I don't know how to thank you other than this," and she handed him a few slips of paper. Andrew stared at them in disbelief. He was holding three tickets to today's baseball game at Yankee Stadium! No one had ever given him something this great, especially someone who did not even know him.

"Please take your parents to the game," she explained. "It's the least I can do for you. I was on my way to work in the stadium offices and you did such a brave thing today."

Andrew couldn't reply. Nobody, not even Jerry, had shown him this much kindness.

"T-thank y-you!" Andrew stuttered finally. He glanced behind him to see the crowd control officer taking the pickpocket with him.

"Well, I have to get to work now," the lady said. "Hurry up to get in line!" She waved goodbye, and set off.

Andrew hurried back in line, only to see the crowd control officer interrogating fans.

"I… had… him, except… he… got… away!" the officer panted. The sight of Andrew made the police officer jump out of his boots.

"You! I meant to talk to you! I have to warn you: You are in danger, son. That thief got away, and I reckon he is after you. Just be alert, will ya'?" Andrew was a bit slow in catching up.

"Okay…"

"Good boy. Now hurry off to your parents. Hold on… where are your folks, eh? I haven't seen them anywhere!"

Andrew's heart lurched and crawled up to his throat.

"Oh… um… my parents? They… work here," Andrew replied weakly.

"Really?" The officer said with a grin. "Well, son. You are in luck. I've got some work to do lookin' for that pickpocket, so I can't see your folks now. But I'm tellin' you – if I ever catch you wandering alone, you're in trouble, mister."

Relief. So much relief. It felt like the weight of the world was lifted off his shoulders.

"Yes ma'am... uh... sir."

With that, Andrew hurried over to the ticket collector. He patted his pocket, just to make sure the tickets were still there.

"Your folks, kid?" a gray haired man at the booth said sternly as he looked at Andrew's ticket. It wasn't a question, but a command.

"They work here," Andrew lied again. The man seemed to have fallen for it.

"Okay, go on in."

Andrew hurried into the stadium, looking at his ticket. "G-4," he muttered to himself. After a lot of walking, Andrew finally found his seat. But he definitely wasn't sitting down. No way.

Sitting in his seat was the pickpocket.

Hide and Seek

*A*ndrew held his breath, slowly backing away. The police officer was right! Andrew knew that the pickpocket wanted revenge.

Just as the pickpocket turned around, Andrew darted off as fast as he could run. Strange faces whizzed by him. Once, he dared to look back, but he thought better of it.

Andrew felt as if he ran around Yankee Stadium – twice. He stopped shortly to catch his breath. Glancing back, he saw the pickpocket turning his head frantically, trying to find Andrew. The object in his hand brought dread to Andrew.

It was a knife. Andrew looked away, trying to forget the image. Andrew shuddered and hurried off.

Desperately, Andrew hurried off to the nearest hiding place – the bathroom. Hiding in a stall, Andrew planned what he would do if the pickpocket happened to find him. Halfway through his 'plan', Andrew realized how stupid that was. Why, on earth, would the pickpocket come in here? Andrew finally came to a conclusion. He was getting out of this stinky bathroom.

Andrew peered through the crack in the stall door. Nobody there. Good. He clicked open the lock and swung open the door.

And froze.

Outside the bathroom, Andrew saw the pickpocket just on the other side of the door. His mind raced frantically. Suddenly, a smirk crept across his freckled face. Andrew hurried over to the mirror, thankful that he never cut his hair. He pulled his thick, blond hair into a ugly pony-tail. Andrew turned around to see the Goth person grinning at him with an evil glint in his eye. His chipped teeth were as yellow as the sun on a hot summer day.

"*Bonjour!*" Andrew said in his best French that he learned from Jerry back at the orphanage. "*Comment allez vous?*"

The pickpocket was bewildered. He knew this kid was not the kid that caught him earlier. "Never mind. Goodbye, French kid."

"*Au revoir!*"

Andrew let out a huge sigh of relief. His plan had worked, and now all he had to do was get back to his seat – not being seen by the pickpocket. He moped out of the lavatory, trying to be inconspicuous.

Though Andrew was glad he wasn't caught, he also was quite disappointed that he had missed most of the game. That lady had spent a zillion dollars for the ticket, and now he put it to waste. He was disgusted with himself.

Hurrying back, Andrew glanced briefly at the scoreboard. The Yankees were up by 4 in the 7th inning. He had missed 7 innings playing 'hide and seek' with the pickpocket.

Andrew got back to his seat; relieved to see no one was sitting in it. He sat back down and waited for the game to end. He guessed that the after the game, he would search the city for another place to stay the night. (Maybe he might even go to the Woolworth Building!) Andrew chuckled to himself.

The game finally ended with a jolt. The Yankees had won it, 7-3. Andrew tried to weave in and out of the rowdy crowds, but it was no use. It was like trying to get through a brick wall. All Andrew could do was wait until the fans had gone past.

Andrew finally made it past the pushy crowds.

And froze. Again.

It was the pickpocket again! He wasn't going to let up! The pickpocket was waiting at the exit. And Andrew had no other choice than to hide in the stadium.

A Night at the Stadium

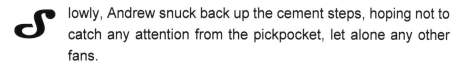lowly, Andrew snuck back up the cement steps, hoping not to catch any attention from the pickpocket, let alone any other fans.

He knew that any quick or false movement would draw the attention of the pickpocket, so he crept slowly until he reached his goal – the bathroom. Andrew hid in the bathroom for what seemed like days. He finally crept out of the bathroom to see the stadium dark and empty. It was nighttime, and Andrew was alone, cold, and hungry. His fingers were as numb as icicles. He decided to search for some leftover scraps of food and a warm place to spend the night.

The cleaning crew is way too good here, Andrew thought to himself. Then he spied an unopened bag of peanuts under one of the metal bleachers.

"Owwww!" Andrew yelled, looking down at his hand. He had split it open on the sharp edge of the metal bleacher. Blood was pouring out of it, while Andrew's mind raced frantically. He ripped off his leather belt and tied it tightly around his hand, stopping the flowing blood. He was able to look up, but not for long. Andrew noticed he had lost too much blood. His vision was getting dizzy, until he dropped to the ground, unconscious.

Andrew woke with a start. It was the middle of the night, and he could hear the noise of screeching cars and the blaring of police sirens. Typical night in New York, he thought.

But then those sounds stopped. And strange ones replaced them. Very strange.

Andrew was rooted to the spot where he stood. His ears could barely take in the sound he was so scared.

It was a voice. Or rather, multiple voices. It sounded like a snake's whisper, slow and hissing. It was a cold, damp, venomous voice. Andrew shivered.

And then it spoke.

"You shouldn't be here, Andrew MacLean… This place gets very spooky at night. It was foolish for you to come here alone. You should have stayed with your friend Jerry at the orphanage." Andrew couldn't speak. His throat was clogged up with fear. Andrew's shirt was drenched with sweat as it spoke again:

"Go home, Andrew."

Andrew just wanted this to be a bad nightmare. He would gasp, and then wake up. But when he pinched himself, he flinched.

It was real.

Now that he knew it was real, he couldn't go home. First of all, he didn't have a home. And second, he couldn't leave here now that there was a mystery to be solved. Who did these voices belong to? How long has this been going on? No, he concluded, he wasn't leaving just yet. He did want to find this out. Ghost or no ghost, Andrew was going to figure this out.

But poor Andrew didn't know was what he was getting into. He was in for a big, scary surprise.

And then he fainted.

A Mysterious Case

*T*he next morning, Andrew got up, rubbing his sore head. He was aching all over, feeling as if a truck hit him. Though his eyes were blurry and his vision wasn't so great, something small and white caught his blue eyes.

It was a baseball.

Andrew ran over to the field, picking up the ball like it was a precious jewel. Staring at it, something popped into his mind. Blast from the Past. The pieces were coming together now!

He remembered what the part of the article in Mr. Baker's drawer had said:

"43-year-old Sean Lockolk reported on seeing an odd type of spirit in Fenway Park yesterday. 'Yeah, it was like a snake hissing. I heard voices, for sure. I was just doin' me job when I heard this voice thing,' says Lockolk. 'At first I thought it was me buddy, Jim. But I knew he don't sound like that. And that's when I heard a loud crack. It sorta sounded like a car backfiring...'" Andrew recited, impressed by his own memory. He dropped the baseball, not knowing what he was doing. So if he was in a stadium, just like that Lockolk person, and he heard the same thing... but how about the crack? Andrew was pretty sure he didn't hear a crack. Andrew decided to wait until nighttime to check it out again. Maybe the voice would come back again tonight!

But as soon as Andrew took two small steps, reality had hit him. He needed to know more information about the crack, and the only way he could find out about it was by reading the actual article. And the article was back at the orphanage.

He had to go back.

Andrew stumbled and sat down. There was no way he could go back to the orphanage, at least not while Jerry was there. He would have to make a plan to go back into the orphanage, steal the article in Mr. Baker's drawer, get back to the stadium, and find out what was making those voices. Too much. But he was going to have to do it. Maybe if he solved the mystery, he would make tons of money and buy a nice place to live. If not, he would go back to living his terrible life with Jerry and Mr. Baker and the rest of the orphans.

He definitely wasn't going to do that.

Andrew set off once again, this time towards the orphanage. He slipped out an open window at the stadium and shimmied down a drainpipe like a firefighter. Hitting the ground with a thud, Andrew took a few steps until the crowd control officer stopped him.

"Well, well, we meet again young fellow. I do recall that the last time we came in touch with each other, I warned you not to be caught wandering around anymore. I'm placing you under arrest," the officer said in a 'poisoned honey' voice.

"No sir. I do have a mom, except she ain't here. Her name is Estella Lewis. Yeah, she's my mom," Andrew lied. "I'm sorry fer' the trouble I caused you, but I gotta' be goin'. Bye!" Andrew hurried off, trying to be out of sight before the police officer noticed anything unusual about that name.

Andrew let out a sigh of relief, and then headed off to the orphanage forgetting about the incident with the officer.

After an hour's walk, the orphanage finally came into Andrew's view. The crumbling walls of the orphanage easily stood out compared to the rest of New York City. But just as Andrew was about to enter the building, he noticed a shadow in Mr. Baker's office, so he thought otherwise. Maybe he won't go in.

At least not with Mr. Baker in his office. He would have to come up with another plan.

Just as he was going to turn around, forgetting all about this, an idea hit him. Oh, he was going to get that article, if it was the last thing he would do.

At least that's what he thought.

Home, Sweet Home

*A*ndrew hurried over to the chain link fence, easily clearing it. He had to find a way to get into the orphanage. He swiveled his head, looking for an opening.

Problem solved.

He ran over to the front door. It was usually locked up tight, but fortunately it was open a smidgen. Wow, he thought, this is easier than he had imagined!

Next task: get the article. This may not be so easy. With his mind clogged up with worries, memories, and ex – best friends, he wondered what Mr. Baker was doing at the moment.

Mr. Baker leaned back in his armchair. He had just finished paying all the bills for the month.

Ah, he thought, life is good. Well, not including the little devil, Andrew. As long as he took care of the article in his drawer, he was fine. But what if Andrew found out about the big secret?

Mr. Baker's mind drifted back to that fateful day many years ago in Boston, when he and his sister Clara made a decision that changed everything. They had no home and barely enough money to eat for one more day. He and Clara entered St. Peter's Church to get warm just as the collection basket was being passed around. At that moment, Mr. Baker and Clara looked at each other and then they both took handfuls of bills. Quickly, they ran out the church. They hid in the alleyways to avoid being caught.

Soon enough, they realized that they had become criminals. The money they stole was not enough to start a new life, so they planned to go back into the church later that night and steal the golden chalice, along with other holy artifacts.

After accomplishing this second burglary, they now had enough money to start a new life. Therefore, they moved to New York City, changing their names to Harold Baker and Gertrude Allard. It looked like they were free and clear to live their new lives until Mr. Baker read the article about the thefts, and how St. Peter's Church would have to close down from the loss of so much money. Unfortunately, there was a description of him and Clara. Then they began to feel somewhat guilty of closing down a Church. The money would be put to good use, they thought. They would use the money they stole to open an orphanage. Surely, this would make up for their sins!

Every so often, Mr. Baker would open his drawer to review the article from many years ago. As long as no one got their hands on it, he and Clara (now known as Ms. Allard) were safe. His mind wandered back into the present, thinking about what to do with Andrew. Should he send the police out to look for him? Nah, he thought. He stroked his mustache. Maybe he should go himself. Or, maybe not. Too much attention to the orphans. Or maybe he could…

"Harold Baker!" came the shrieking voice of Ms. Allard. "What have you been doing to my papers?!" Mr. Baker shot up out of his chair like a cannon, quickly locking the article in his desk. He definitely didn't recall messing up anyone's papers. He lumbered over, his round belly jiggling as he ran (he actually waddled, rather than ran). Unfortunately, he'd left the keys to the drawer (and his lunch) on his desk.

Big mistake.

Andrew MacLean hurried off to Mr. Baker's office, leaving a pile of Ms. Allard's papers on the ground. He peeked in, just in case Mr. Baker happened to still be there.

Nope.

He leaped in, grabbing the keys on the desk. Even with his trembling hands, he was finally able to get the drawer open. There it was! Gently, he picked it up, leaving the drawer open. He was about to leave when something stopped him.

Andrew turned around and grabbed Mr. Baker's lunch just for good measure.

Now, he could leave.

Mr. Baker hurried back to his office after cleaning up the mess he didn't make. He opened the door. And he stopped cold.

The drawer was half – open, and the article was gone! Even his lunch was gone! His chubby fingers trembled at the sight. His heart seemed to stop. He dropped to his knees, letting out a wail. In a second, Ms. Allard stood beside him, scolding him about how foolish he looked.

"No, Gertrude, you don't understand! That Andrew MacLean boy…"

"Yes, what about him? He's gone and that's all I care! Now can I get back to work? My students are waiting very patiently!"

"Gertie, he KNOWS THE SECRET!!! He took the article!"

"Harold, do you know what this means?" Ms. Allard said, horror-struck. "What are we going to do? We could go to jail!"

"Yes!" he cried. "We need get the article back!"

By now, Andrew was already back in the stadium. How quickly he figured out how to get in just by climbing the drainpipe and going into the window, which was left open. He glance behind his shoulder, just to make sure nobody followed him. Positive he was alone, he sat down in a bleacher and read the article out loud to himself:

"… 'car backfiring. I checked the sky to check fer' lightnin', but there weren't nuthin'. Jim did the same thing. We looked at each other, then we ran, 'cause on the field were a couple of ghosts. I dunno if it was me eyesight or what, but it was weird.'" Andrew leaned back into the hard metal seat. Ghosts? He wasn't sure about that. But he'll find out, sooner or later. He lay down, thinking about what time it was. Probably about 6:20 or so. In order to wait until the voices came again, he would just have to get some rest. But when he woke up, he planned to figure out the mystery.

Andrew's eyes were glued on the field wearily. The field was tossing and turning just like Andrew, until his eyes drooped shut.

Impossible

*A*ndrew's eyes opened a millimeter. It was dark out, so he knew he didn't sleep too late. He got up, shaking his head, his hair flying like a shaggy lion's mane around him. He felt as anxious as a kid about to receive a birthday present. The sky was painted black with smog and clouds.

Suddenly, out of the blue, Andrew saw a wisp of smoke. His head jerked in the direction of the field.

Nothing.

Disappointment. Andrew began to think that this wasn't even real. Anyway, there was no such thing as ghosts! They don't exist! How does he know that Sean Lockolk was telling the truth? If he was...

"Andrew... Andrew... why do you doubt us? We are very real... very." Andrew whipped his head just in time to see pearly white glowing figures on the baseball field. They were wearing Yankees uniforms.

"You know, Andrew, we are not alive in flesh, my boy. We are soul. Pure, pure soul." Andrew was rooted to the spot, shaking. Another voice spoke. "Do not be scared, Andrew MacLean. We only appear to those in need of our help, so I say to you, do not run away from your problems. Deal with Jerry, face to face." Andrew seemed to calm down a bit, though he was curious about who was speaking.

Then it came to him.

It was Babe Ruth, along with other Yankees legends.

Andrew gasped. No, he thought, this was impossible. Ruth and his teammates had died decades ago!

"Oh Andrew... yes, I am Babe Ruth, and yes, we are dead. But why don't you believe that I am here?" he said expressionless. He seemed to be reading Andrew's mind!

"S-sir... um..." Andrew stuttered in a small voice. "I don't get it. One night you say go h-home, then the n-n-next night y-you give me advice!" Babe let out a hearty laugh.

"I now know that you do believe in me, one way or another. Others have approached me totally skeptical. None except you can see me, Andrew. Lad, I say to you: Go home. You can't live here much longer. Gertrude Allard and Harold Baker are looking for you as we speak."

Andrew cursed under his breath. He knew those two would come after him!

"Andrew, do not tell anyone about us," a kind voice said. Andrew recognized it as Lou Gherig's. "None will believe you." Andrew stared.

The ghosts, (or 'spirits'), had taken positions on the field, and they started playing baseball! He stood there, gawking. His mind had basically shut down completely.

Suddenly, a loud crack rang out through the stadium. Andrew perked up. A glowing baseball had sailed over the front row bleachers and plopped down gently right next to Andrew.

No bouncing, no noise. It lay there, as if it were dead. It was a miracle.

Old Friends

*A*ndrew picked the ball up with amazement. His fingers felt numb on its cool surface. He turned it around in his palm; names were etched upon it.

All the Yankees stars had signed it.

Just as he was about to say, "Thank you," the ghostly voice echoed, "Goodbye, Andrew. Good luck." And then all was silent, except the noisy honking of cars.

Andrew stood there, rooted to the spot, until the horrible truth dawned upon him.

He was going home.

Well, not exactly, seeing as he didn't have a home. What he meant was that he was going back to the orphanage to stay.

Stay. That word sent shivers down Andrew's spine. But yes, his adventure was over, and so he would go back 'home' in the morning. He yawned and leaned back, his stomach grumbling.

And he would need some food, too. Andrew smiled and went to sleep.

"C'mon, boy. Wakie-wakie time. Yo' mammy ain't gonna be too happy, y'know." Andrew's eyes popped open. The baseball was under his stomach, prodding into him. At least it was safe.

But he wasn't.

"Now, ain't it time to pay ya back fer' costin' us that lady's wallet? I think so. Ain't that right, Snakie?"

"Yup."

Andrew was staring wide – eyed into the faces of the pickpocket, along with his 'friends'.

"Oh yeah," the pickpocket said sarcastically. "Before we beat up the little runt, I say we give the kiddie our names. It musta' been hard fer' you, not knowin' our names. Well, I'm Fang, this one here is Snakie, the fat one's Chub, and the tall and skinny one is Pizza." He gestured to each one of them with his tattooed arm, beads jingling.

Andrew was frozen to the spot. All he could do was hold the base-ball tight, not letting any of them get a hold on it. Should he run? Nah, they would catch him.

Suddenly, the fat one, 'Chub', spoke.

"Eh, Fang, don't ya think we shoulda' just beat 'im befer' he woke up?"

"Hah! It's called scaring 'im. I like it betta' 'at way." They closed in on him, hands outstretched.

Andrew did what came to the top of his mind. He ran.

He dashed over the damp bleachers, around candy booths, through aisles, and onto the field. Andrew glanced back only to see Fang, Snakie, and Pizza following him. Chub stopped by the candy booth, breaking into it, devouring all he saw.

Just as Andrew was near left field, he tripped. Out of all the things he could have done, he tripped. There was nowhere he could go. He was trapped.

Suddenly, a flash of light made his eyes squint. The field was covered with mist. Thick, heavy, and dark. He could hear the pickpocket and his gang swearing and cursing at the top of their lungs.

Now was his chance. He darted off, back up onto the bleachers.

Chub turned around, his chin covered with candy and their wrappers. He lunged at Andrew, missing him by an inch. Andrew heard a thud and a lot of screaming coming from Chub. Back to business, he thought, just get out of here.

In no time, he was out of the stadium. The spirits just saved his life by slowing down the gang. And the baseball was still safely in his pocket. He patted it, only to have a look of fear cross his face.

The pocket was empty.

Andrew sprinted back to his entrance to the stadium, which now seemed to have been destroyed. Fang's work.

"Hey, you boy! Come back here!" Andrew whipped his head around.

A uniformed police officer was yelling at him, holding a club. Stupidly, Andrew raised his hands above his head, showing the officer that he had nothing dangerous on him.

"What do y'think you're doin'?" the officer snarled, gripping Andrew's shoulder tight enough to break his bones.

"No, officer, you don't understand! There are these other robbers."

"Other robbers?" the police officer interrupted, growling. "I've been in this service 22 years, and I'm too old to believe in coincidences. All I know is that you're here, and the entrance to the park is burnt through. Ever hear of the word 'arrest'? Just gonna' tell you, you'll be hearing that word a lot." Andrew stared into the cold eyes of the police officer for a few minutes before speaking up again.

"Uh, sir, could you let go of my shoulder... yeah... um... it is starting to hurt."

"Kid, get in the ca..." his voice trailed off, leaving his eyes staring over Andrew's shoulder.

"What in the world..." Andrew turned around to see Fang, Snakie, Pizza, and Chub all with shocked expressions etched upon their faces.

"Well, well... so it may be that this young lad was tellin' the truth." The police officer strutted over to them and grabbed one of their wrists dangling with jewels. "Either me eyes are getting' old or this is the same thief that took my wife's bracelet. Interesting, interesting..." He gestured to another police officer to help him.

"C'mere, Sergeant, help me take these rascals to the station. As fer' the boy... just pop him in the car, too." Andrew obediently followed the Sergeant to the police cruiser. Unwillingly, he sat down next to Pizza, who gave him a nasty look. Fortunately, they had handcuffs on.

"Okay, son, where is your mom an' pop?" The Sergeant spoke for the first time. Andrew had been dreading that question for a long, long time. But he would have to tell the truth, sometime.

"Uh, sir, I don't really wanna' talk right know... y'know, I would really like some private space..." The Sergeant, who Andrew found out his name was Steven, glanced at him suspiciously from the front seat of the car. Andrew turned back around, his eyes locking on Pizza's pocket.

It was the baseball.

New Friends

*A*ndrew held his breath, glancing at Pizza's face. Good. He hadn't noticed. Pizza and Snakie were grumbling and swearing to each other, muttering about how idiotic the officers were. Andrew's hand crawled silently into Pizza's pocket, grabbed the baseball, crawled out, and placed the baseball back into his own pocket.

And Pizza didn't even notice.

"Well, we might as well deal with you before we go anywhere with these four. Where is your house? We, Sergeant Steven and I, need to talk to your folks. You live…"

"New York City orphanage," Andrew mumbled weakly, seeing Fang snicker. "It is on Branche Street. You know, near the Liquor store? It's run by Ms. Allard and Mr. Baker."

"Yeah. I know that. Kid, why didn't you say you were an orphan?"

Andrew hesitated and kept quiet.

Finally, after what seemed like hours, they arrived at the orphanage.

"Captain, you stay in the car. Look after these criminals. I'll bring in..."

"Andrew," he interrupted. Andrew was tired of them calling him 'kid'.

"Fine. I'll bring in Andrew." Steven explained. Andrew hopped out of the car, following the Sergeant. Maybe I should run away, Andrew thought.

"Oh, um, officer?"

"Yes?"

"I... sorta' took this from Mr. Baker's office in the orphanage," Andrew explained, handing over the article. The Sergeant stared at it, and then stuffed it in his pocket. Slowly, the officer kept walking, his face smeared with confusion and curiosity.

He knocked on the screen door, taking a few steps back behind Andrew. The door opened with a clatter as a high voice (which Andrew recognized as Ms. Allard's) pierced the cool air.

"What is it?"

"Ma'am, do not speak to a Sergeant like that. Let me in." Andrew closed his eyes, trying to forget what might happen next.

"Oh, um, sorry. Come in…" Ms. Allard spoke shrilly, startled by her mistake. She stepped aside, letting Andrew and the Sergeant enter. Andrew tried not to make eye contact with Ms. Allard, but he could already tell that she was glaring at him with her narrowing eyes.

"This boy, Andrew, was found wandering the streets of New York all alone. Is that true?"

"Yes, officer."

"Why didn't you report him missing? Is this how you run your orphanage?"

"Oh no officer," Ms. Allard said timidly. "We do everything we can to keep all the orphans safe. There must have been a mix up. It won't happen again, officer." But Andrew knew she was lying, and the Sergeant seemed to think so, too.

"Andrew, honey, please go back to your dorm," Ms. Allard said way too sweetly. Andrew obeyed her, galloping up the creaky stairs.

"Will that be all officer…" was the last thing Andrew heard before entering his dorm.

Jerry was sitting on a bed, reading The Swiss Family Robinson. He looked up and a surprised look found its way onto his face.

"Is that you, Andrew?"

"Yup."

"Where have you been? Why did you leave?" asked Jerry.

Andrew sat down beside Jerry. "What happened between us? We were great friends, and then all of a sudden, mortal enemies," explained Jerry. "I felt so alone and I thought you didn't care. Andrew – nothing was the same when you left. I'm sorry. Can we just forget everything and become friends again?"

Andrew came over to Jerry, sticking out his hand. "Buddies?"

"Oh, yeah." And they shook on it.

They both laughed, and a ball rolled out of Andrew's pocket.

"What is that?"

"Er... nothing. Well, it was sort of a gift someone gave me." He didn't want to hurt Jerry's feelings, so he paused. Luckily, Jerry spoke up, breaking the awkward silence.

"Hah! That's okay. Anyway – who would want a plain old baseball?"

"Well," Andrew began. "It's not a plain old baseball. See, look. It was signed by the Yankees legends. There is Joe Sewell, that one is Lou Gherig, oh, and I think this one's Tony Lazzeri, and, that one is Babe Ruth! Can you imagine that? Babe Ruth!" Jerry just stood there, unmoving.

"Andrew!" Jerry exclaimed. "Where on earth did you get this? It's probably worth 'bout a million bucks!"

"Jerry, I think we should hide this, y'know. If Baker sees it, he'll take it in a blink of an eye."

Just as they were about to hide it, the shrieking voice of Ms. Allard rang through the orphanage. "Andrew! Get down here. We have to talk," Ms. Allard yelled.

Andrew hurried down the steps with an odd sense of curiosity. "Yes?"

"I want you to explain to the officer and me why and how you left. Immediately." Andrew hesitated, and then began. He told them the truth; for he was quite tired of lying. Andrew explained how he got out, and how he stumbled upon the stadium. On and on he went, retelling his bold adventure. Finally, when he was finished, Ms. Allard stood there, horrified.

"Hello, everybody," a new voice cheered merrily. Andrew turned around to see Mr. Baker covered with food and sauce. "So, Gertie, when's suppa'? I've been starving like a wild animal. Why is MacLean here? I thought he was gone! Gertie, what happened?"

Ms. Allard's pale face looked as white as a ghost.

At that moment, the Captain entered with a stack of papers and asked to talk to the Sergeant quietly. Ms. Allard and Mr. Baker allowed them, but their faces were painted with fear.

When they finished talking, the Sergeant took out two pairs of handcuffs, telling Ms. Allard and Mr. Baker that they were under arrest for robberies in Boston and for using false names. He had connected them to the crimes in Boston from their descriptions in the article Andrew had taken from Mr. Baker's drawer.

The officers started to take them away, when Andrew piped up, "But what will happen to the orphanage?"

Sergeant Steven explained that Mr. Point, the Science teacher, had agreed to take over temporarily until the city of New York can find a permanent replacement for Mr. Baker and Ms. Allard.

After the officer led Mr. Baker and Ms. Allard off to jail, Mr. Point gathered the kids in the cafeteria to explain what happened.

"…and so, the policeman has appointed me to take over the job."

A New Beginning

*L*ife at the orphanage was so different under Mr. Point. He hired a painter to repaint the peeling gray walls of the orphanage. He hired a new cook who actually could cook quite well. Best of all, he cared for the orphans.

"Andrew, my boy, would you mind giving me a hand with this turkey? Arthritis is my biggest enemy these days," said Mr. Point, gesturing toward the 25-pound turkey.

"Yeah … sure," Andrew replied nervously eyeing the huge turkey. "Why don't I go get Jerry to help us move the turkey," said Andrew.

"That would be great!" exclaimed Mr. Point.

Andrew bounded up to his dorm, finding multiple orphans decorating the halls for the big Thanksgiving dinner the next day.

"Jerry?" Andrew called.

"What?" Jerry answered back.

"C'mon. Mr. Point needs us to help move the turkey into the kitchen." Jerry nodded, hurrying down the steps.

"Thank you, gentleman," Mr. Point commented as the three heaved the turkey into the kitchen, which was filled with the aroma of freshly baked apple pie.

Monsieur Marcel Lessard, the new cook, rushed over to them. "*Merci, monsieurs!*" Marcel Lessard thanked them, sliding the turkey onto the counter. "This turkey looks *très bon!*" Mr. Point looked bewildered. It was obvious that he did not speak French.

"*Au revoir!*"

Andrew and Jerry headed back up to their dorm. "Ya know," Andrew said thoughtfully, "I kinda like it here now. I mean, with Mr. Baker and Ms. Allard gone, I feel like we are almost in a real home."

"I feel the same way," Jerry stated, "but I still would rather have a real family. I mean who wouldn't?" Andrew sighed.

"You're right, but let's just focus on what we have to do now, with all the holidays coming up."

"Okay," Jerry nodded. There was so much to do to get ready for tomorrow's big feast, the rest of the day passed quickly.

Thanksgiving was finally upon them and before they knew it, they were holding hands all around the table with the scrumptious feast.

"Dear Lord, we thank You for this food You have given us through the kindness of Your loving heart. We thank You for all of us around this table and help us to always be grateful for what we have," Mr. Point prayed.

"Amen," rang through the room. All of a sudden, as if someone flipped a switch from "OFF" to "ON", the orphans were chatting and indulging themselves with all the food in front of them.

It was the best Thanksgiving Andrew and Jerry had ever had. It felt like home – well, almost.

The next day, Andrew and Jerry were all excited about the upcoming holiday, Christmas. They were helping Mr. Point put up decorations in the entrance hall of the orphanage.

"Andrew," said Mr. Point. "Do you have a …."

Ding-Dong.

"I wonder who that could be at the door now?" Mr. Point murmured. He ambled over to the door and opened it.

Andrew's jaw dropped.

A New Family

S tanding in the doorway was Estella Lewis, the lady who had given Andrew the tickets for the baseball game, along with a handsome man in a wheelchair. Andrew couldn't believe it. "Is that you, Mrs. Lewis? Its great to see ya' again!" She smiled and greeted him warmly.

"I didn't know you lived here. It is so nice to see you again. I don't even know your name," said Mrs. Lewis.

"My name is Andrew, Andrew MacLean. I'm sorry I didn't mention to you that I didn't have a family when you gave me the tickets to the Yankees game over the summer."

"Jake, this is the boy I told you about. He got my wallet back from a pickpocket," commented Mrs. Lewis. "If only I had known you didn't have a family, Andrew, I could have done more to help you."

"Andrew, let the poor lady in," said Mr. Point. Obediently, Andrew did what he was told, letting in Estella and the man in the wheelchair.

"Thank you, sir. My name is Estella Rose Lewis, and this is my husband, Jake Lewis." Estella explained to Mr. Point. "We have met with Mr. Baker a few times earlier this year and we have an appointment today to formalize an adoption of one of the children."

"Welcome, Mr. and Mrs. Lewis. It is a pleasure to have you here," Mr. Point said cheerfully. "I was unaware of the meeting you had scheduled today with Mr. Baker. Mr. Baker left the orphanage quite suddenly this summer and I have been appointed as the new director. I am still getting used to my new position. Why don't we go into my office to discuss the adoption," said Mr. Point.

Mr. and Mrs. Lewis entered Mr. Point's office, leaving Andrew and Jerry dumbfounded in the hallway.

"I'm so glad to hear that you want to adopt one of the children here!" Mr. Point exclaimed once he and the Lewis' were back in his office. "I apologize for not being familiar with your case, but Mr. Baker's filing system was not quite complete. Had you gotten to the point where you had selected a child to adopt?"

"Our meeting today was for us to meet some of the children and get to know them, but we already know who we are adopting," Mrs. Lewis said as she looked over to her husband. "His name is Andrew MacLean."

Mr. Point was pleased. "Andrew is such a nice boy. He has not had it easy here, but he has a good heart. He will be a wonderful addition to your family. Would you like me to have him come in so you can tell him the great news?"

"Absolutely," said Estella and Jake at the same time.

"Thank you so much, Mr. and Mrs. Lewis!" Andrew said politely after hearing the news. Andrew tried hard to contain his excitement since he did not want to ruin his chances to have a new family.

As the Lewis' went over to Mr. Point's desk to sign some papers, Andrew ran into the hallway to tell Jerry.

"...and now she's signing the papers! Can you believe it?!" Andrew exclaimed. Jerry's facial expression didn't look too happy.

"That's great, Andy. Congrats. But the thing is that we won't be together anymore. Y'see?" Jerry said nervously. Horror struck Andrew. Jerry was right! He would have to tell Mrs. Lewis.

"Hold on," Andrew demanded. "I think I can fix this." He ran back into Mr. Point's office.

"Mr. and Mrs. Lewis, I can't be adopted. I just can't," Andrew explained. Estella looked confused.

"Why?"

"Cause I can't leave Jerry here. He's my best friend. We're practically brothers and I just could not be happy knowing that Jerry was here alone." Stella glanced at Jake. He nodded, saying,

"Well, why not? I suppose he can come with us too, under one condition."

"What?"

"You love us."

"I think we can manage that," Andrew replied, grinning. "Lemme go tell Jerry."

"Okay. Don't be long!"

Andrew ran out of the office once again, telling Jerry the whole story.

"We're gonna' be real brothers! Cool, ain't it?"

"Yup."

"Jerry, can you wait a sec, I gotta' ask Estella, I mean… Mom… some questions. Bye, bro."

Andrew ran back into Mr. Point's office.

"Mrs. Lewis, Jerry says he's fine with it. Now I gotta' ask you a major question: Why do you want to adopt me?"

"Andrew, the first time we met, I liked you and felt the need to protect you. My husband and I always wanted children but after his accident, we could not have children of our own. We had so much we wanted to give to a child; we decided to adopt a little boy. When I saw you again today, it seemed like fate. We feel we are meant to be your parents."

Andrew heard Jerry enter Mr. Point's office. He saw Estella, and froze.

"U-um, nice to meet you, er, ma'am."

"Mom."

"Yeah. Mom."

"Come on, you two. Why don't you go gather up your things and we can all head home," Stella said.

"I like the sound of that," Andrew and Jerry said at the same time.

News of the adoption traveled fast throughout the orphanage and soon enough all the kids in the orphanage knew that the pretty lady and the guy in the wheelchair were adopting Andrew and Jerry.

Once Andrew and Jerry had all their belongings, they were met in the hallway by Mr. Point and all the other kids from the orphanage.

"Goodbye!" chorused Mr. Point along with the children. Andrew was sure that he would not see them anytime soon.

"Bye!" Andrew and Jerry replied for the last time. They looked at each other, smiling broadly.

"Jinx!" They both laughed and headed out the doorway.

For good.

EPILOGUE

C hristmas arrived early that year, and the two brothers were merrily singing Christmas carols while their parents trimmed the tree.

"Andrew, dear, do you mind handing me the star?" inquired the mother standing tall on a step-stool. The young boy joyfully obeyed his mother, handing her the shimmering star.

"Beautiful," the mother commented. "just beautiful." The small family of four stood back, admiring their work.

"Mother," one of the boys said. "can we go to bed early? I want to be able to sleep before Santa comes." The mother looked at her husband, grinning.

"Oh, yes. Up to bed, you two." The two boys galloped up the steps.

"Night mom and dad, love you."

"Good night."

The boys crawled into their puffy beds, smiles ear to ear. It would be a long night.

The next morning the boys woke to the smell of freshly baked cinnamon rolls their mother had cooked. They ran downstairs, yelling for joy. They ripped open their presents with excitement.

"Okay, Andrew, Jerry, we have a special gift for you both," the mother and father said together, arms interlocked.

"Really? What is it?"

"Oh, you'll find out."

The two boys rushed over to the kitchen, yelping once they saw a large, square box. Ripping one corner, one of the boys screeched,

"It's a dog!"

"No way!"

"Really!"

The mother was delighted with her sons' glee.

"Hey, mom and dad," the boys chorused.

"Yes?"

"We got you something too."

The mother smiled.

"Okay. What is it?" The boys handed her a small box. She opened it slowly, as if wanting to savor this moment. Her pale jaw dropped as she took out a million dollar baseball.

"Jake, dear, look at this!" Her husband wheeled over. He stared at it, his mouth hanging open.

"Where did you get this?"

"Oh," the boys said, "and old friend gave it to Andrew, but now we want you to have it."

"I promise, Andrew and Jerry, we will treasure this for the rest of eternity," the mother said admiringly. "But about the dog..."

"What are you gonna' name it, Andrew?" the father asked. The blond haired boy glanced at his brother.

"How 'bout Ginger," he said, admiring his new golden retriever.

"That's a nice name," commented his father. "What do you think, Jerry?"

"I like it."

"Then Ginger it is." Jerry trotted over to the living room.

"How about a Christmas story, mom?" he prodded to his mother.

"I don't see why not."

"Wait 'till Andrew comes, 'cause I know he loves stories, too," he said eyeing his brother, who was now hugging his new dog. Jerry smiled at him and gestured him to come into the living room. They all sat down on a couch as a family. A real family.

About KidPub Press

KidPub is devoted to helping kids develop their writing skills by giving them a safe, fun, supportive place to express their creativity. At KidPub we know that kids have lots of creative ideas and plenty of stories to tell.

In addition to our web site, we publish books, like this one, written by kids ages eight to fourteen. You can find many more books to enjoy, written by young authors, at our online bookstore.

Thousands of visitors come by each day to read the stories posted by our members and to post their own writing. We invite you to visit Kid-Pub to browse our books, read new stories, and find out how you can publish your own book with KidPub Press. We're on the web at www.kidpub.com.

Made in the USA
Lexington, KY
17 July 2010